OWEN'S WALK

Text copyright © 2006 by Karen Hill.

Illustrations copyright © 2006 by Carol Thompson.

All rights reserved. No portion of this book may be reproduced in any form without the
written permission of the publisher, with the exception of brief excerpts in reviews.

Published in Nashville, Tennessee, by Tommy Nelson®, a Division of Thomas Nelson, Inc.

Visit us on the Web at www.tommynelson.com.

Tommy Nelson® books may be purchased in bulk for educational, business, fund-raising,
or sales promotional use. For information, please email SpecialMarkets@ThomasNelson.com.

Scripture quotations noted as (ICB) are from the International Children's Bible®, New Century Version®,
© 1986, 1988, 1999 by Tommy Nelson®, a Division of Thomas Nelson, Inc. All rights reserved.

Scripture quotations noted as (NIV) are from the Holy Bible, New International Version®.
Copyright © 1973, 1978, 1984 by International Bible Society. Used by permission of
Zondervan Publishing House. All rights reserved.

Special thanks to Chuck Wallington for encouraging me to cut paths for my grandchildren.

Library of Congress Cataloging-in-Publication Data

Hill, Karen, 1947–
    Owen's walk / written by Karen Hill ; illustrated by Carol Thompson.
        p. cm.
    Summary: Using a picture book which depicts Bible verses, Owen tries to find his way
through the woods to his father's house.
    ISBN 1-4003-0694-9 (hardback)
    [1. Christian life—Fiction. 2. Allegories.] I. Thompson, Carol, ill.
II. Title.
    PZ7.H55283Owe 2006
    [E]—dc22
                                                    2005012900

Printed in China

06 07 08 09 10 — 9 8 7 6 5 4 3 2

FOR OUR OWEN—
MAY YOU ALWAYS WALK WITH THE SAVIOR.

OWEN'S WALK

KAREN HILL

ILLUSTRATED BY
CAROL THOMPSON

A Division of Thomas Nelson Publishers
Since 1798

www.thomasnelson.com

"Is it ready?" Owen called as he raced into the kitchen, the screen door flap-flapping behind him. The boy washed his hands, then gave his grandmother a half-hug before plopping down on the thick phone book that rested on his chair.

Mimi smoothed her apron with flour-dusted fingers. She leaned over the oven door to retrieve a loaf of crusty bran bread. "It's ready!" she said.

Owen liked having a special spot at his grandmother's table. It felt good to know where he belonged and that his place was always ready for him.

"Tell me about your morning," Mimi urged as she brought Owen a hot, buttery slice of bread.

"Okey-dokey," Owen said between bites. "I went to my favorite place— the barn. . . .

First, I gave Ol' Hobo some oats,

and then I made a pirate ship out of the hay bales,

and then I found the mama cat—she has three new kittens! And then . . ."

"Goodness, you've been a busy boy!" Mimi said with a smile.

"Mimi, you have the best farm in the whole wide world. I wish I could stay longer."

"I know," Mimi said in her gentlest voice, "but we'll see each other again soon."

Owen scooped up the last breadcrumb and popped it into his mouth.

"What's all that stuff?" he asked, pointing to a jumble of items on the counter.

"I'm packing some things for your adventure."

"Adventure?" Owen asked.

"Sure. It will be more fun if you think of your journey as an adventure," Mimi said as she filled Owen's backpack with a harmonica, a belt, a small spade, a jar, and a key.

Mimi continued packing. "A lunch, breadcrumbs for the squirrels, and this. It's the most important of all," she said, reaching for a brown leather book.

"What's that?" Owen asked.

"It's *The Book of Signs*." Mimi opened the book to the first page and read,

"This book is for Owen
To help you on your way.
Be careful and watchful,
And on the path you'll stay."

Mimi sat down with Owen, and they looked through the book together. "The pictures in this book will remind you of a Bible verse you've learned. When you are unsure about your journey, pull out this book. *The Book of Signs* has the answers you'll need."

Owen hesitated. "But . . . Mimi, I've never gone by myself. What if I get lost? I'm just a kid, you know."

"Don't be afraid. You have everything you need to get home. Your father went ahead to make a path for you. Just stay on your father's path, and you'll get along fine."

The two stepped onto the back porch. Mimi held the backpack as Owen weaved his arms through the straps.

Owen started up the trail that would lead him through the woods. He turned and waved to his grandmother.

"Love ya!" he called. And as he headed toward the trees, he heard her familiar response, "Love ya back!"

And so began Owen's walk.

At first the trail was familiar. Just beyond the mountain laurels was the live oak with Mimi's wind chimes in its branches. One time she had stirred the chimes with a stick, as if conducting a grand orchestra. "Sometimes you have to make your own music," she had said.

Now a breeze stirred the chimes. The music floated along the path with Owen as he continued down the trail.

Soon Owen came to Mimi's "listening bench." He sat down to watch and listen to the world of the woods. A bird tweeted a happy song. A rabbit hopped out of its underground house. A squirrel skittered near Owen's feet.

"Hey, little buddy, are you hungry?" Owen asked, tossing a handful of crumbs to his forest friend. Then Owen continued down the path.

Owen hadn't gone very far when the path split into two trails. Unsure which path to take, he remembered his grandmother's words, "*The Book of Signs* has the answers you'll need." He pulled out the soft leather book.

On the first page, Owen saw two signs. One was a crooked arrow pointing to the left. The other was a straight arrow pointing to the right.

"I know," Owen said, "stay on the RIGHT path." The boy smiled and took the path to the right.

It wasn't long before Owen heard a sound coming from the deep woods. It was coming closer—it sounded like an elephant stampeding toward him. Quickly, Owen crawled into a smelly, old hollow log, just big enough for one boy and a full backpack.

Owen turned to the next page in *The Book of Signs*. He saw a picture of a child with his guardian angel nearby.

"That's right. I don't have to be afraid," Owen said. "God's with me everywhere I go." When he peeked out, he was surprised.

It was a deer! Owen wriggled out of his hiding place and dusted himself off.

"Here, little deer, I won't hurt you," he said. The deer stood still, watching the boy. Owen pulled the harmonica out of his backpack and began to play his favorite tune for the deer.

His concert finished, Owen loaded up his backpack and continued his journey.

Owen liked everything about the deep woods—the crunch of the leaves under his feet, the plop of acorns falling to the ground, bugs going about their day. But suddenly . . .

Owen tripped and tumbled into a
deep ditch. Covered in dirt and leaves,
his elbow scraped and sore, Owen worried.
"There's no one here to help me out of
this ditch."

He turned another page in *The Book of Signs* and saw a picture
of a strongman's arm. "God will make me strong. He will
help me."

"God, please help me," Owen prayed as he reached into his
backpack and found the belt Mimi had packed. Holding one end
of the belt, Owen tossed the other end over the branch above,
and then looped it through the buckle. Now he could pull
himself back up to the path.

Owen continued on his way until he came to a brook. . . .

How could he cross the water?

"I didn't know adventures could be so tough," Owen said to himself. "But Mimi always says, 'A problem is a chance to show God that you trust him to be your helper.'"

Once again Owen opened *The Book of Signs*. He found a picture of a big rock. "God is my rock. I can go to him."

Owen looked around. "That's it. Rock steps!"

He took the small spade and dug up two large, flat rocks. He threw them into the brook. Then Owen leaped from the edge of the brook to the first rock, then onto the next, and finally to the path on the other side.

Owen began to run. He didn't slow down until the sun began to slip behind the treetops and long, dark shadows covered the path.

He opened *The Book of Signs*. The next picture showed a bright light shining out of darkness. "God will give light to my lamp."

Just then Owen noticed lights flickering through the trees. "Lightning bugs!" He took the jar from his backpack and opened it. The blinking bugs floated into the jar. "Now I have a lantern to light the path!"

Finally, up ahead a bright light glowed. It was the light of . . . "Home!" Owen shouted.

Light poured out of every window. Lanterns blazed on the front porch. Owen's father stood in the open doorway.

Key in hand, Owen unlocked the gate and raced to his father. "Dad! I made it! I followed *The Book of Signs* and stayed on the path!"

Dad smiled.

Owen was home, safe in his father's arms.

Owen's Adventure Backpack

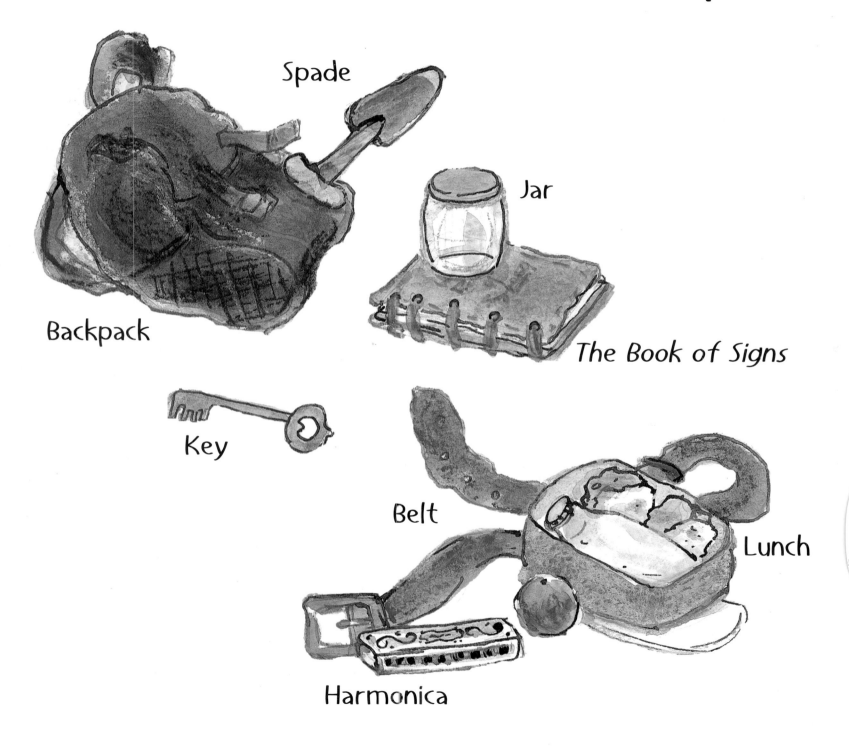

Spade

Jar

Backpack

The Book of Signs

Key

Belt

Lunch

Harmonica

Mimi's House

Owen's Walk
The Path Home

Commit your way to the LORD; trust in him.
—Psalm 37:5 (NIV)

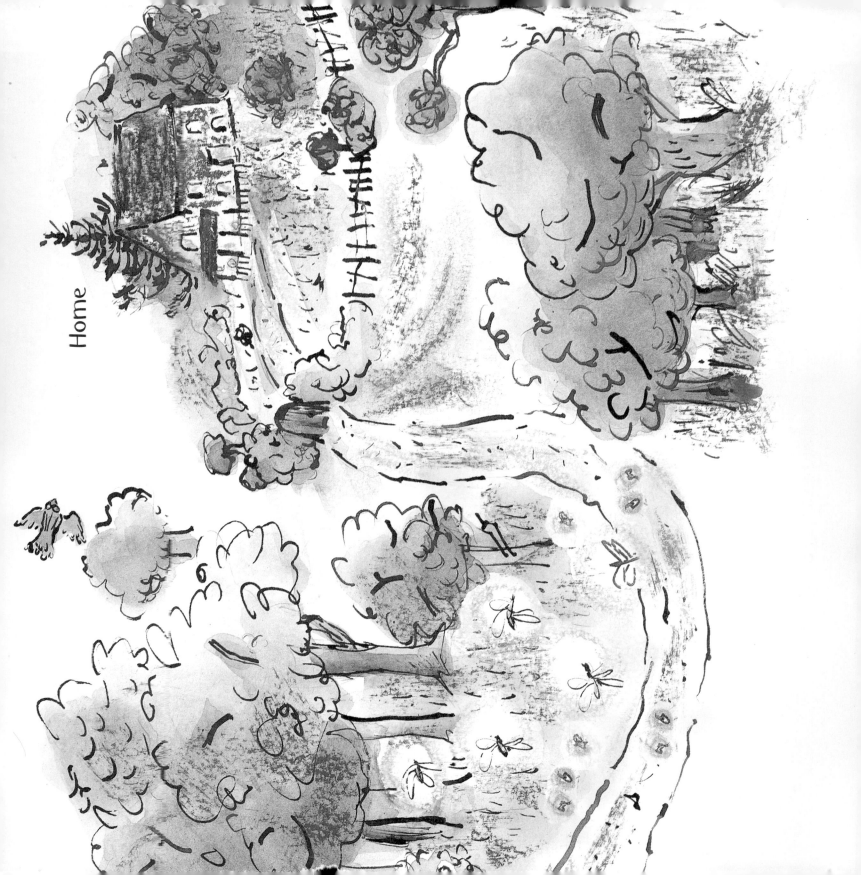

Home

The Book of Signs
with Bible Verses

I am your God. I will make you strong and will help you.
—Isaiah 41:10 (ICB)

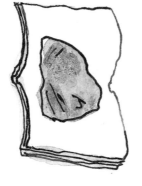

My God is my rock. I can run to him for safety. He is my shield and my saving strength, my high tower.
—Psalm 18:2 (ICB)

...ten, my son, and be wise, and keep your heart on the right path.
—Proverbs 23:19 (NIV)

...t be afraid. The Lord your God will
...e with you everywhere you go.
—Joshua 1:9 (ICB)

Lord, you give light to my lamp.
—2 Samuel 22:29 (ICB)